CHOCOLATE FEVER

by
Robert Kimmel Smith

Student Packet

Written by
Jean Jamieson

Contains masters for:

1	Pre-reading Activity
6	Vocabulary Activities
3	Poetry Writing Activities
1	Matching Activity
8	Writing Activities
1	Chocolate Frosting Dough Activity
7	Math Activities
1	Spelling Activity
2	Illustration/Art Activities
1	Research Activity
1	Conclusion Activity
1	Teacher Suggestions for Assessment
1	Comprehension Quiz

PLUS   Detailed Answer Key

Note

The text used to prepare this guide was the Dell Yearling softcover, copyright @ 1972 by Robert Kimmel Smith. If another edition is used, page references may vary.

ISBN 1-56137-703-1

To order, contact your local
school supply store, or—

Novel Units, Inc.
P.O. Box 791610
San Antonio, TX 78279

Activity: Reading for information

Chocolate

Chocolate is a nutritious confection. It possesses a pleasing and widely popular flavor and also ranks high in food value. Chocolate contains carbohydrates, fats, protein and several vitamins and minerals. Many people whose work requires physical endurance, including soldiers, explorers and athletes, rely on chocolate as a source of quick energy for carrying out their tasks.

Milk chocolate probably ranks as the most popular of all chocolate products. Chocolate liquor, whole milk solids and granulated sugar are the basic ingredients in this form of chocolate. Extra cocoa butter, obtained from cocoa powder production, is added to the chocolate liquor. First the ingredients are mixed well. Then the mixture passes through a series of large steel roll refiners. The shearing and rubbing action of these rolls reduces the mass to a smooth paste. Machines called conches then process the chocolate for 72 hours. In these machines, a large cylindrical stone rolling on a stone bed pushes the chocolate back and forth. This rubbing action smooths off any rough edges on the chocolate particles, helps to develop the desired flavor, and finishes blending the entire mass. Milk chocolate is sold in the form of bars and as the coating on some candies.

Sweet chocolate and semisweet chocolate are processed in the same way as milk chocolate. However, manufacturers do not add milk solids to the mixture in making these products. Manufacturers sell large amounts of both sweet and semisweet chocolate to confectioners for making chocolate-covered candies. Increasingly large amounts of semisweet chocolate are used to make homemade cookies, candy, cakes and other items.

Read the following statements. Mark each statement either T (true) or F (false).

_____ 1. Chocolate is a nutritious confection.

_____ 2. Milk chocolate is not the most popular of the chocolate products.

_____ 3. There are no milk solids in semisweet chocolate.

_____ 4. People whose work requires physical endurance often rely on chocolate.

_____ 5. Chocolate does not contain carbohydrates and fats.

Name _____

Activity: Word recognition, grouping of letters into words, extending knowledge regarding the use of chocolate

Chocolate Word Search Puzzle

Do the word search. Write down the letters that have not been used, starting at the top and working left to right in each row. Group letters into words to finish this sentence:

HENRY GREEN EATS _____.

```
B  R  E  A  D  P  U  D  D  I  N  G  M  P  C  F
R  A  C  F  U  D  G  E  C  C  C  P  I  U  C  I
O  C  V  A  L  H  O  C  R  E  O  I  L  D  U  L
W  L  R  A  R  U  O  L  E  C  O  N  K  D  S  L
N  A  O  E  R  A  F  T  A  R  K  W  S  I  T  I
I  E  W  G  A  I  M  F  M  E  I  H  H  N  A  N
E  C  A  K  E  M  A  E  S  A  E  E  A  G  R  G
S  M  I  L  K  I  P  N  L  M  S  E  K  L  D  T
H  M  I  N  T  E  V  I  C  E  R  L  E  A  R  M
Y  T  E  G  G  N  O  G  E  R  S  S  H  Z  O  O
M  E  R  I  N  G  U  E  A  T  E  I  A  E  P  U
C  H  I  F  F  O  N  P  I  E  S  A  L  U  S  S
B  O  N  B  O  N  S  S  Y  R  U  P  M  K  C  S
I  N  G  E  C  L  A  I  R  S  O  U  F  F  L  E
```

BAVARIAN CREAM	BREAD PUDDING*	BROWNIES	ICING
CAKE	CHIFFON PIES	DROPS	COOKIES
FILLING	CREAM PIE	CUSTARD	ECLAIRS
EAT	EGGNOG	FLUFF	FUDGE
ICE CREAM	MILK SHAKE	MOUSSE	PINWHEELS
PUDDING*	SAUCE	SOUFFLE	SYRUP
BONBONS	CARAMEL	MERINGUE	CREAMS
GLAZE	MINT	MILK	SILK
LOG			

*Please note that this puzzle asks for pudding and bread pudding. Please do not circle the pudding in bread pudding for the pudding in the first column.

Activity: To write a limerick

Henry Green

"The truth was that Henry was in love with chocolate. And chocolate seemed to love him."
(page 16)

A *limerick* is a five line poem with a specific rhythm. The first, second and fifth lines rhyme. The third and fourth lines rhyme. The fifth line of a limerick is often written with a humorous twist. Write a limerick or other poem about Henry Green.

My Limerick About Henry Green
Henry Green thought that chocolate was neat
And sometimes it was all he would eat.
He would eat it all night
Till his face was a sight
And sometimes even his feet.

Your Poem About Henry Green

_____ 1

_____ 2

_____ 3

_____ 4

_____ 5

Activity: To read and to learn

Marco Polo

"Mark Green was ten and tall and very good to Henry. He only got angry when Henry called him Marco Polo." (page 15)

Match each READ statement to the LEARN statement that completes the thought by drawing a line from the READ statement to the LEARN statement. Example follows:

READ	LEARN
1. Marco Polo was an Italian trader and traveler.	a) More than three years after leaving Venice, they reached Kublai Khan's summer palace in Shangdu.
2. He was raised by an aunt and uncle. They trained him to be a merchant.	b) The Polos' journey to China and back probably totaled nearly 15,000 miles. The men were gone 24 years.
3. In 1271, when Marco Polo was 17, he sailed to Palestine with his father and uncle.	c) He became famous for his travels in Asia and China.
4. The Khan made Marco a government official in China. He served many years.	d) The book helped bring to Europe such Chinese inventions as the compass, papermaking and printing, as well as the use of coal as fuel, paper money, and a postal system that used a network of courier stations.
5. Marco Polo wrote a book about his travels. *Description of the World* had to be copied by hand as printing had not yet been invented in Europe.	e) Besides learning reading, writing, and arithmetic, Polo learned about using foreign money, judging products and the handling of cargo ships. He also became conversant in four languages.

Activity: To follow directions

Chocolate Frosting Dough

"If there was one thing you could say about Henry it was that he surely did love chocolate."
(page 17)

Object of Activity: To follow directions to make Chocolate Frosting Dough

WASH HANDS BEFORE STARTING ACTIVITY

Materials:
1 can chocolate frosting
1 1/2 cups powdered sugar
1 cup peanut butter
spoon
bowl
piece of foil or waxed paper, approximately 9 inches by 12 inches in size
newspaper

Process:

1. Cover the work area with newspaper.
2. Place materials on the the newspaper.
3. Mix all ingredients in bowl with spoon.
4. Place mixture on the foil or waxed paper.
5. Knead mixture into workable dough with hands.
6. Model as with any dough.
7. This dough is edible.
8. Clean up work area.

Activity: To create a recipe for an unusual chocolate concoction

Recipe

"Can you imagine a boy having a chocolate-bar sandwich as an after-school snack?" (page 17)

Henry seems to try a form of chocolate with everything that he eats. He might enjoy trying the following recipe:

Grilled Chocolate Sandwich

2 slices any type of bread
soft butter or margarine
one to two milk chocolate candy bars

1. Spread soft butter or margarine on one side of each bread slice.
2. Place milk chocolate candy bars* between bread slices, buttered sides OUT.
3. Grill slowly on both sides until chocolate has melted and bread is golden brown.
4. Serve warm. (*Peanut butter may be added with the chocolate before grilling.)

- -

Make up an unusual chocolate recipe for Henry to try. Illustrate your recipe with a picture of how the item will look when ready to eat.

_____

_____

_____

_____

_____

_____

_____

_____

_____

_____

Activity: To use mathematics skills

Chocolate Kisses

"Henry went through the kitchen and gathered a handful of chocolate kisses to put into his pocket. He liked to have them handy to munch on at school." (page 19)

Here are some interesting facts about chocolate kisses:

   a) 33 million chocolate kisses can be produced in one day.

   b) There are approximately 95 chocolate kisses in one pound.

   c) There are 25 calories in each chocolate kiss.

Use the information given about chocolate kisses to answer the following questions:

   1. How many chocolate kisses can be produced in 5 days?

   2. What is the approximate weight of one chocolate kiss?

   3. Approximately how many calories does one pound of chocolate kisses contain?

   4. If one pound of chocolate kisses cost $3.00 (and if you can buy just one at that rate), how much would one chocolate kiss cost? (Round up to next cent.)

Activity: To use writing skills

Something Is Going To Happen

"I have the feeling something's going to happen, and I don't know what." (page 21)

You decide what will happen. Change the story at this point by adding something unexpected to Henry's day.

_____

_____

_____

_____

_____

_____

_____

_____

_____

_____

_____

_____

_____

_____

_____

_____

_____

_____

_____

_____

_____

Activity: To use mathematics skills

Fractions

"At the front of the room, Mrs. Kimmelfarber was going through the drill on fractions." (page 22)

For this activity you will need a fun size bag of plain chocolate dot candies.

    1. Remove the candy pieces from the bag.

    2. Count the candy pieces. Total number of pieces in the set. _____

    3. Sort the candy pieces by color. Make a record of how many are in each color set.

        Dark Brown   _____

        Orange   _____

        Green   _____

        Red   _____

        Yellow   _____

        Tan   _____

    4. Write the fraction for each color, telling how many of the total set is dark brown, orange, green, red, yellow and tan.

       For example: In my fun size bag of chocolate dots there are 26 candy pieces. There are:

       3 tan, 4 green, 2 orange, 3 yellow, 7 dark brown and 7 red. OR
           3/26 of the set of candy pieces are tan
           4/26 of the set of candy pieces are green

       Record your fractional data here:

Activity: To learn different lyrics to a song; to use mathematics skills

Little Brown Spots

Henry said, *"Little brown spots all over. I was looking at my arm and I have these."* (page 24)

The following lyrics may be sung to the tune of the song "Ninety-nine Bottles of Pop."

Twenty-one brown spots on his arm
Twenty-one brown spots.
If eleven more come on out   **21 + 11 = 32**
Henry has thirty-two brown spots on his arm.

Thirty-two brown spots on his arm
Thirty-two brown spots.
If eleven more come on out   **32 + 11 = 43**
Henry has forty-three brown spots on his arm.

Continue the song, adding eleven brown spots for each verse. Do the calculations for each verse. **How many spots** will you add in three minutes?* _____
(Use a separate sheet of paper to record your calculations.)
* Use a three-minute egg timer if available.

Change the numbers in the verse. For example: Start with 33 spots and add on 7.
Thirty-three brown spots on his arm
Thirty-three brown spots.
If seven more come on out
Henry has forty brown spots on his arm.

1. _____
_____
_____
_____

2. _____
_____
_____
_____

Name _____

Activity: To become a magician by using prose or poetry

Chocolate Milk

"Mr. Pangalos' round nose twitched, and he sniffed the air. 'Chocolate?' he said. 'Have they brought the chocolate milk upstairs already?' " (page 28)

Use prose or poetry to change something that is outside into chocolate milk, and describe what happens.

(Examples of things to change: a concrete road into a road of chocolate milk; rain drops into drops of chocolate milk; waterfall into a cascade of chocolate milk, etc.)

_____
_____
_____
_____
_____
_____
_____
_____
_____
_____
_____
_____
_____
_____
_____
_____
_____
_____
_____

Activity: To think of words that may be used to describe feelings

Feelings

"Henry felt as if his heart were about to drop into his shoes." (page 28)

Use each letter of Henry's name as the first letter of a word that may be used to describe a feeling. For example: The **H** may be used as the first letter of the word **Happy**.

H _____

E _____

N _____

R _____

Y _____

G _____

R _____

E _____

E _____

N _____

What one word describes how you feel today? _____

Activity: To make a list of words that are associated with sound

Pop!

"What is that noise, then? It sounds like something going pop." (page 31)

Make a list of all of the words that you can think of that have something to do with sound, such as the word **pop**.

POP
BANG
CRACK

Use ten of the words from your list in descriptive sentences. (For example: The new shoes squeaked across the hard wood floor.)

(Use the back of the page if necessary. Thank you.)

Name _____

Activity: To use the letters of one word to form others; spelling practice

Mrs. Kimmelfarber

"Mrs. Kimmelfarber and Henry rush through the door that morning." (page 29)

How many words can you make from the letters in the name MRS. KIMMELFARBER in three minutes? Compare your list of words with another member of the group. Can you make longer lists by working together? Try it.

FAR   _____   _____
BAR   _____   _____
MAR   _____   _____
_____   _____   _____
_____   _____   _____
_____   _____   _____
_____   _____   _____
_____   _____   _____
_____   _____   _____
_____   _____   _____

How many words can you make from the letters in the name MOLLY FARTHING in three minutes? Work with a partner. Make a list.

FAR   _____   _____
MAR   _____   _____
GAR   _____   _____
_____   _____   _____
_____   _____   _____
_____   _____   _____
_____   _____   _____
_____   _____   _____

Activity: To create an original tongue twister

Chocolate Chips

"His little brown spots were growing bigger and bigger. No longer the size of freckles, they were as big as the chocolate bits his mother used for making cakes and cookies." (page 33)

Use the words **Chocolate Chips** and other words beginning with **ch** to create your own tongue twister.

Tongue twisters are rhythmic patterns of language which use clusters of similar sound.

Start out with a short tongue twister. Practice saying that, increasing the speed without making an error. To make the tongue twister more of a challenge, increase the number of words, one at a time.

For example:

CHIC CHOCOLATE CHIPS

CHOICE CHIC CHOCOLATE CHIPS

CHOSEN CHOICE CHIC CHOCOLATE CHIPS

Your Tongue Twister:

_____

_____

_____

_____

_____

_____

_____

_____

_____

_____

Activity: To use the imagination

Candy Bar

"Chocolate. Those big brown spots are pure chocolate. The boy, it seems, is nothing more than a walking candy bar!" (page 40)

Make a cartoon that shows a person as a walking candy bar. Write a caption to go with the cartoon. Use a candy wrapper, if available, to represent the candy bar.

Activity: To make a cost comparison

Candy Bar Cost

Compute the cost per pound of the following candy bars. (When figuring the cost per ounce, round up to the next cent.) Add candy bars to the list if you know the price and the weight of each bar.

Formula: cost per pound = price/weight in ounces x 16
(note: 16 ounces = 1 pound)

Candy Bar	Weight in Ounces	Price	Cost Per Pound
A	1.45 ounces	50¢	
B	2.31 ounces	50¢	
C	1.76 ounces	50¢	
D	2.15 ounces	50¢	
E	1.6 ounces	50¢	
F	1.875 ounces	50¢	
G	1.69 ounces	50¢	
H	2.1 ounces	50¢	
I	1.85 ounces	50¢	
J	2.07 ounces	50¢	

See next page.

Activity: To use graphing skills

Candy Bar Cost
(Continued)

After the cost per pound has been determined for each candy bar, **make a bar graph of the results**.

Make summary statements about the graph. Include statements that answer the following questions: Which candy bar has the **highest** cost per pound? Which candy bar costs the **least** per pound? Which candy bars have the **same** cost per pound?

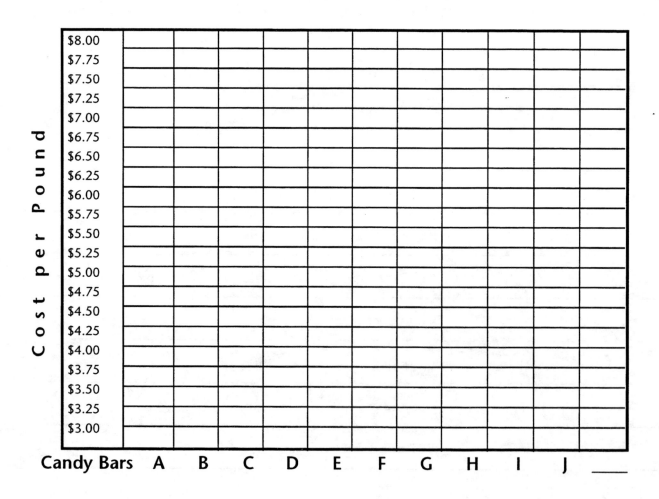

Activity: To write a detailed, descriptive report

Dr. Fargo

"All kinds of doctors were examining Henry now, poking and prodding as if he were not a boy, but a pincushion." (page 41)

Imagine that you are Dr. Fargo and that you have to write a report about this new disease. You must describe the symptoms and test results and make recommendations about treatment for the patient. Give as much information as possible.

Report

Name of patient _____ Date _____

Symptoms:

_____
_____
_____
_____
_____

Test Results:

_____
_____
_____
_____
_____

Recommendations:

_____
_____
_____
_____

Signed _____ (For Dr. Fargo)

Name _____

Activity: To alter one circumstance in a situation

A New Disease

"...Dr. Fargo was bounding about the room, talking about 'Chocolate Fever'...'a new disease'...'making medical history'...and things like that." (page 41)

What if Henry loved a different food as much as he loves chocolate? (For example: peanuts or peanut butter, pickles, mustard, catsup, spaghetti, meat loaf, strawberries, lemon, etc.)

Change the food, which will result in different symptoms and "a new disease." **Write a short story** about Henry, and make illustrations for it. (Use additional paper for your work.)

_____
_____
_____
_____
_____
_____
_____
_____
_____
_____
_____
_____
_____
_____
_____
_____
_____
_____
_____

Activity: To write a cumulative story rhyme

Run! Run!

"There was a whole army of people pursuing Henry. Doctors in white coats, nurses, guards blowing whistles, policemen waving their arms. And behind them Henry could see Dr. Fargo."
(page 44)

In the tale of *The Gingerbread Man*, the Gingerbread Man said:
Run, run as fast as you can.
You can't catch me, I'm the gingerbread man.

Create a rhyme about Henry that is similar to the tale of the gingerbread man.

Make at least one **illustration** for your rhyme. Use additional paper.

For example, the following starts one version of Henry's tale:

Henry ran down the street;
Policemen running pell-mell.
As they ran, they heard Henry yell—

"Walking, running, or even by car,
You can't catch me,
I'm the boy-chocolate-bar!"

Now, policemen and guards
hot in pursuit,
With Henry yelling while giving a salute.

"Walking, running, or even by car,
You can't catch me,
I'm the boy-chocolate-bar!"

Activity: To write an original cheer; to teach the cheer to others

Surrounded!

"In less time than it takes to tell about it, Henry was surrounded." (page 49)

Change how the boys react to Henry. Imagine that they want to make Henry feel better about himself.

Make up a cheer for the boys to say to Henry. When finished, teach your cheer to a few of the group members. Say the cheer for others. If you know of someone in need of the cheer, change the name and say it to that person.

My Cheer For Henry

Henry! Henry!
Don't feel blue.

Henry! Henry!
We care about you.

YOUR CHEER FOR HENRY

_____

_____

_____

_____

_____

_____

_____

Activity: To use antonyms to bring about change

UGLY!

"One of the tallest boys, who looked a good deal older than Henry, spoke up. 'Boy, are you ugly!' he said." (page 49)

Henry is described by some of the boys in the group surrounding him as:

Descriptive Words Used:	**One Antonym: (opposite)**
UGLY	_____
HORRIBLE	_____
DISGUSTING	_____
REVOLTING	_____
NAUSEATING	_____

"The more the boys called him names, the worse Henry felt. He opened his mouth to say something, but nothing came out." (page 50)

Write an antonym for each word next to it. **Do not repeat a word** used as an antonym.

How do you think Henry would feel if the boys substituted the antonyms of the descriptive words?

Write about Henry's reaction to the antonyms.

Activity: To create a chocolate dream

From the Bunk

"After sitting alongside Mac for an hour or so in the front seat, Henry had climbed up to the bunk and fallen quickly asleep." (pages 57 and 58)

Imagine that you are Henry, asleep in the bunk of the truck. You are having a Chocolate Dream. In your dream everything you see is made of something chocolate! (For example: chocolate ice cream bushes, chocolate cake houses, etc.)

Use prose or poetry to **paint a picture with words** as you describe Henry's dream.

Henry's Chocolate Dream

DESCRIBED BY _____

_____

_____

_____

_____

_____

_____

_____

_____

_____

_____

_____

_____

_____

_____

Activity: To use mathematics skills

Suppertime

"Mac reached down below his seat and brought up a big picnic basket. He placed it between them on the seat." (page 59)

Calculate the cost of a meal on the road if Mac had to stop to purchase food for the two travelers. First make choices if Mac had **unlimited funds**, and then if he had **$10.00**.

Choose from the selections given below for both Mac and Henry. Calculate the cost for each person as well as the combined total. What would you order from the menu? What would be the total cost for your food?

Food Item	Price	Cost for Henry	Cost for Mac	Combined Cost
6 inch submarine sandwich	$1.99 each			
fish meal (potato & green beans)	$2.99 each			
chicken planks & fries	$1.99 each			
roast beef sandwich	$1.69 each			
chicken sandwich	$1.69 each			
2 piece chicken dinner	$1.99 each			
pasta & breadsticks	$1.99 each			
cheeseburger, fries & drink	$3.99 each			
gyros sandwich	$3.49 each			
large pizza, 2 toppings	$9.99 each			
large beverage, your choice	89¢ each			
apple	69¢ each			
bag of potato chips	59¢			

TOTAL COST_____

Name _____

Chocolate Fever
Student Worksheet #25
Chapter 9

Activity: To make a comparison using a synonym or an antonym

Vocabulary Review

Use the following vocabulary words in this activity:

CONCEIVABLE   CLIMAXED   WACKY   PECULIAR
IRRESISTIBLE   CAUTIOUSLY   RIDICULOUS   REVOLTING
DECLINED   UNFORTUNATE   GLUMLY

Complete each of the following comparisons by using one of the vocabulary words.

Sample: GOOD is to BAD as HOT is to COLD.

1. PITIFUL is to PATHETIC as _____ is to POSSIBLE.
2. GOOD is to KIND as _____ is to PEAKED.
3. LARGE is to SMALL as _____ is to SANE.
4. BETTER is to WORSE as _____ is to NORMAL.
5. SCARED is to FRIGHTENED as _____ is to OVERPOWERING.
6. MARVELOUS is to WONDERFUL as _____ is to CAREFULLY.
7. HERE is to THERE as _____ is to SENSIBLE.
8. GLAD is to HAPPY as _____ is to DISGUSTING.
9. FIND is to LOSE as _____ is to ACCEPTED.
10. LIKED is to DISLIKED as_____ is to FORTUNATE.
11. COMMON is to SPECIAL as _____ is to HAPPILY.

Make up two of your own comparisons. You do not have to use vocabulary words.

(a) _____

_____

(b) _____

_____

Activity: To compare prices; to calculate value

The Last Laugh

"With Mac's laughter ringing in their ears, the unhappy thieves looked glumly ahead as the truck rumbled through the night." (page 71)

At the onset of this adventure, the thieves think that the truck is loaded with furs. Much to their dismay, they find out that Mac has a load of candy bars in his truck.

However, if Mac's truck were filled with different candy, the value of the haul would change.

Calculate the value for the following candy. (When figuring the cost per ounce, round up to the next cent.)

Type of Chocolate Candy	Weight	Cost	Cost per pound	Value 25,000 lbs.
Chocolate Bars	1.45 ounces	50¢	$5.60	_____
Molded Solid Chocolate	3 ounces	$3.95	_____	_____
Chocolate Mints	5.5 ounces	$7.00	_____	_____
Chocolate Hearts	6 ounces	$8.00	_____	_____
Chocolate-covered Strawberries			$15.95	_____
High-priced Chocolates	12.5 ounces	$50.00	_____	_____
Estate Chocolates			$15.00	_____
Your Favorite Boxed Chocolates	_____	_____	_____	_____

Activity: Interpretation and explanation

Trust

"Henry would follow Mac's lead and do as he was told. The big man was a person you could trust, especially in a tight spot." (page 73)

A **proverb** is a short, popular saying that expresses some obvious truth.

Read the following proverbs. Choose the one that you think says something about Mac. Tell what the proverb means to you. Make an illustration for your explanation on the back of the page or on a separate sheet of paper.

A friend in need is a friend indeed. English

A good friend is better than silver and gold. Dutch

Trust everybody, but thyself most. Danish

A word of kindness is better than a fat pie. Russian

Kindnesses, like grain, increase by sowing. English

A little for you and a little for me—this is friendship. East Indian

Where friends, there riches. German

Courage beats the enemy. Philippine

Courtesy is compatible with bravery. Mexican

My Choice: _____

What the proverb means to me:_____
_____
_____
_____

Name _____

Activity: To match a vocabulary word with its definition

Vocabulary Crossword Puzzle

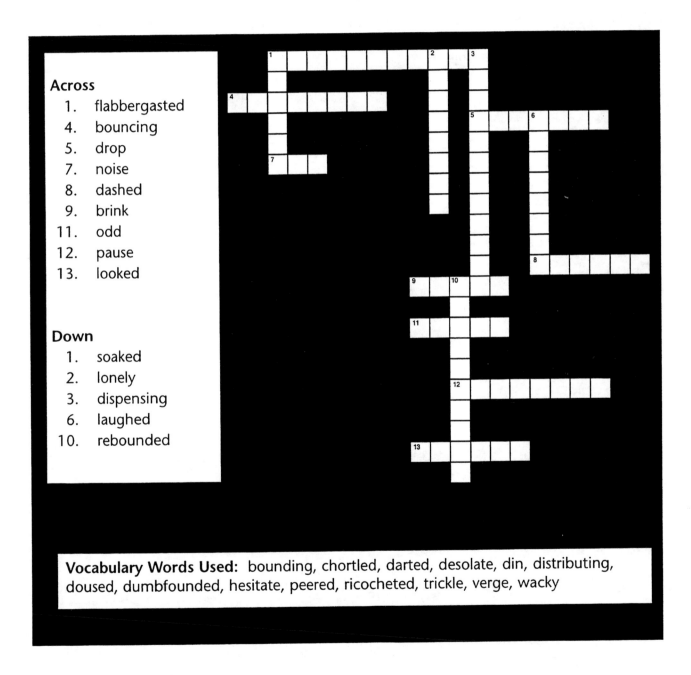

Across
1. flabbergasted
4. bouncing
5. drop
7. noise
8. dashed
9. brink
11. odd
12. pause
13. looked

Down
1. soaked
2. lonely
3. dispensing
6. laughed
10. rebounded

Vocabulary Words Used: bounding, chortled, darted, desolate, din, distributing, doused, dumbfounded, hesitate, peered, ricocheted, trickle, verge, wacky

---

Activity: To make a collage

Products

"Imagine seeing every kind of candy bar, cookie, and cake all in one spot." (page 82)

Object: To make a Chocolate Collage

A **collage** is an artistic composition made of various materials glued on to a surface.

Materials: newspaper, shirt cardboard or a piece of a box, glue, colored pictures of things made with chocolate from magazines and other print media, ribbon, candy liners, candy wrappers, small candies like red cinnamon hearts, etc.

Process:

    a) Cover work area with newspaper.

    b) Put materials on newspaper.

    d) Arrange colored pictures and candy wrappers on the cardboard, to cover it.

    e) Glue pictures onto cardboard.

    f) Arrange ribbon, small candy liners and wrappers and small candies on top of the pictures.

    g) When pleased with the arrangement, glue in place.

    h) Let glue set before moving collage to drying area (about 15 minutes).

    i) Clean up work area.

    j) Make up a title for your collage.

    k) Display your work.

Name _____

Activity: Vocabulary word recognition, grouping of letters into words and word usage

Vocabulary Word Search Puzzle

Do the word search. Write down the letters that have not been used, starting at the top and working left to right in each row. Group letters into words to find out what is so unique about Henry that he makes medical history.

He has the _____ of Chocolate Fever.

```
P  R  E  D  I  C  A  M  E  N  T
H  U  I  N  F  I  R  M  A  R  Y
E  B  R  I  L  L  I  A  N  T  O
N  O  E  S  U  B  S  I  D  E  D
O  U  C  U  U  N  I  Q  U  E  I
M  N  A  R  M  I  R  T  H  N  E
E  D  L  V  I  L  N  I  F  Y  S
N  I  L  I  C  G  A  G  O  S  E
O  N  E  V  E  R  G  E  I  T  L
N  S  P  E  C  T  A  C  L  E  S
```

WORDS TO FIND	
PREDICAMENT	PHENOMENON
SURVIVE	BRILLIANT
INFIRMARY	UNIQUE
BOUND	RIOT
FOIL	RECALL
PURSUING	SUBSIDED
DIESEL	SPECTACLES
VERGE	RIG
DIN	MIRTH

Some other things to do:

1. Put the words in alphabetical order.

2. Define every other word.

Activity: To read for information

Cinnamon

"Henry wondered how cinnamon would taste on what was left of his stack of pancakes."
(page 91)

Cinnamon is a popular spice used in cooking and for flavoring candies and preserves. It comes from the inner bark of the cinnamon tree. The tree grows in Sri Lanka, the principal source of the spice, and in Brazil, India, Jamaica, Java, Madagascar and Martinique.

The cinnamon tree grows as high as 30 feet and has oval leaves and tiny yellow flowers. The fruit of the cinnamon tree looks like an acorn. Workers cut off the tops of the cinnamon trees near the lower buds so that strong, straight shoots grow up from the base. The shoots are gathered, and the inner bark is peeled off. The bark then turns brown and curls up as it dries. The dried bark is sold as stick cinnamon or is ground up to make powdered cinnamon.

Oil of cinnamon is made from the fruit, leaves, and roots of the tree. An oil similar to that of the cinnamon tree comes from a related plant, commonly called cassia. Cassia oil and bark are often used instead of cinnamon.

Information Source: Information Finder, 1994 World Book, Inc.

_____

Read the following statements. Mark each statement either T (true) or F (false).

_____ 1. Cinnamon comes from the inner bark of the cinnamon tree.

_____ 2. Cinnamon is not a popular spice used in cooking.

_____ 3. Sri Lanka is the principal source of cinnamon.

_____ 4. Cinnamon also comes from Brazil, India, Jamaica, Java, Madagascar and Martinique.

_____ 5. Stick cinnamon is the dried, curled bark of the cinnamon tree.

_____ 6. Oil of cinnamon is made from acorns.

_____

Sugar Cane reminds Henry that "we can't have everything we want every time we want it!"

As the story ends, Henry is not eating chocolate, but is wondering if there is such a thing as *Cinnamon Fever.*

What is your opinion of the situation? Do you think that Henry has learned a lesson about overdoing a good thing, or will he start all over again? Why do you feel as you do about Henry?

_____

_____

_____

_____

_____

_____

_____

_____

_____

_____

_____

_____

_____

_____

_____

_____

_____

_____

_____

_____

_____

_____

_____

To The Teacher:

The concluding activity may be used as the final test of the novel unit.

The student is asked to state an opinion regarding Henry's state of mind as the story ends, and to give reasons for coming to that conclusion. Has Henry, in fact, "learned his lesson?"

The following pages may be used as quiz pages if the teacher so desires:

a) Pre-reading, Worksheet #1, Chocolate. Reading for information.

b) Chapter 1, Worksheet #2, Chocolate. A word search puzzle for word recognition and the grouping of letters into words.

c) Chapter 1, Worksheet #4, Marco Polo. To read, learn, and recognize complete thoughts.

d) Chapter 3, Worksheet #12, Feelings. To think of words that may be used to describe feelings.

e) Chapter 4, Worksheet #13, Pop! To make a list of words that are associated with sound; to use some of the words in descriptive sentences.

f) Chapter 4, Worksheet #14, Mrs. Kimmelfarber. To use the letters of one word to form others; spelling practice.

g) Chapter 7, Worksheet #22, Ugly! To think of antonyms for some specific words.

h) Chapter 9, Worksheet #25, Vocabulary Review. To make a comparison using a synonym or an antonym.

i) Chapter 10, Worksheet #27, Trust. Writing activity emphasizing interpretation and explanation.

j) Chapter 11, Worksheet #28, Vocabulary Crossword Puzzle. To match a vocabulary word with its definition.

k) Chapter 12, Worksheet #30, Vocabulary Word Search Puzzle. Vocabulary word recognition, grouping of letters into words and word usage.

Comprehension Quiz follows.

Name _____

Read the following information. Fill in each blank space with a word, words, or phrase that will make the information given complete and true to the story.

1. Henry Green loves the flavor of _____.

2. Henry's little brown spots become as big as _____.

3. Dr. Fargo determines that Henry is a walking _____.

4. Henry gets away from the boys in the schoolyard by telling them that if they touch him they _____.

5. Mac, the truck driver, is very _____ to Henry. Mac even shares the supper in his _____with Henry.

6. The truck is _____ before Mac and Henry can make a _____ to Henry's family.

7. The hijackers think that the truck is full of _____. It is really full of _____.

8. Because Henry smells like _____ , Mac and Henry are able to get away from the _____.

9. Mac and Henry deliver the candy to a man named _____ ,who once had _____ himself.

Answers

Worksheet #1
1. T
2. F
3. T
4. T
5. F

Worksheet #4
1. c
2. e
3. a
4. b
5. d

Worksheet #7
1. 165,000,000 kisses
2. 0.1684 oz.
3. 2375 calories/pound
4. 4¢ a kiss/$0.0316

Worksheet #2
CHOCOLATE Word Search: HENRY GREEN EATS
CHOCOLATE WITH EVERYTHING

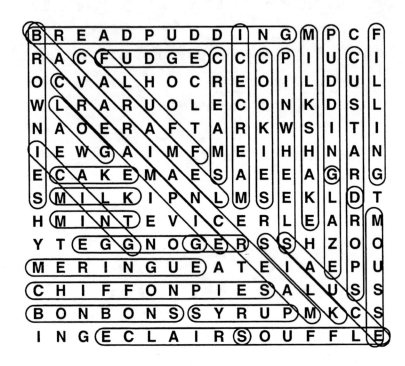

Worksheet #12 (sample answer)
Happy
Excited
Nice
Rambunctious
Yucky

Giddy
Relieved
Energetic
Ecstatic
Naughty

Worksheet #13
Some examples of words associated with sound:

pop	clank	pat
bang	crash	rap
crash	clack	drum
snap	click	strike
clap	jingle	smack
flash	tinkle	exhale
burst	ring	blow
clatter	chime	whistle
rattle	jangle	honk
jangle	tap	hiss

38

Worksheet #14 (sample answers)
MRS. KIMMELFARBER:

far	lame	rake	flake	fair
bar	same	lake	fare	milk
mar	blame	sake	rare	silk
mask	firm	make	mare	silk
ask	bare	bake	film	blare
bask	bear	fake	air	are

MOLLY FARTHING:

far	art	hot	from	lag
mar	mart	got	firm	rag
gar	thing	rot	form	tag
rat	ring	toy	lay	nag
hat	fling	golly	ray	hag
mat	not	folly	gay	fan

Worksheet #17, page 1
Candy Bar Cost
Note: The price per ounce was figured, rounding up to the next cent, and then multiplied by 16 to find the cost per pound.

A $5.60 per pound
B $3.52 per pound
C $4.64 per pound
D $3.84 per pound
E $5.12 per pound
F $4.32 per pound
G $4.80 per pound
H $3.84 per pound
I $4.48 per pound
J $4.00 per pound

Worksheet #22
Some antonyms for **UGLY**:

UGLY: pretty, attractive, handsome, beautiful
HORRIBLE: agreeable, fascinating, enchanting
DISGUSTING: attractive, delightful, alluring, captivating, delectable
REVOLTING: pleasing, agreeable, attractive, charming
NAUSEATING: pleasing, delightful

Worksheet #25

1. CONCEIVABLE
2. CLIMAXED
3. WACKY
4. PECULIAR
5. IRRESISTIBLE
6. CAUTIOUSLY
7. RIDICULOUS
8. REVOLTING
9. DECLINED
10. UNFORTUNATE
11. GLUMLY

Worksheet #26

Note: The price per ounce was figured, rounding up to the next cent, and then multiplied by 16 to find the cost per pound. The per pound cost was then multiplied by 25,000 to find the value of 25,000 pounds.

Chocolate Bars $140,000.00
Molded Solid Chocolate $528,000.00
Chocolate Mints $512,000.00
Chocolate Hearts $536,000.00
Chocolate Covered Strawberries $398,750.00
High-priced Milk Chocolates $1,600,000.00
Estate Chocolates $375,000.00

Worksheet #28

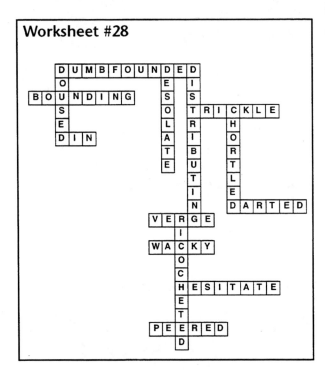

Worksheet #30

He has the ONLY CASE of Chocolate Fever.

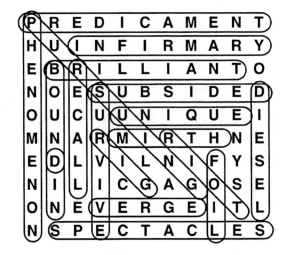

Comprehension Quiz

1. chocolate
2. chocolate bits or chips
3. candy bar
4. will die
5. nice or kind—picnic basket
6. hijacked—telephone call
7. furs—candy bars
8. chocolate—hijackers
9. Alfred Sugar Cane—Chocolate Fever

Worksheet #31

1. T
2. F
3. T
4. T
5. T
6. F
